Disney DESCENDANTS 3

WELCOME TO

AURADON

ACTIVITY AND STICKER BOOK

BY BILL SCOLLON

BASED ON THE FILM BY
JOSANN McGIBBON & SARA PARRIOTT

Disney PRESS
LOS ANGELES · NEW YORK

Copyright © 2019 Disney Enterprises, Inc.

Manufactured in the United States of America
First Paperback Edition, October 2019
1 3 5 7 9 10 8 6 4 2
ISBN 978-1-368-04955-9   FAC-029261-19165

For more Disney Press fun, visit www.disneybooks.com
Visit DisneyChannel.com

WELCOME TO AURADON

Welcome to the United States of Auradon, a beautiful country made up of many legendary kingdoms. The capital is Auradon City—the place to be in the land of ever after. It's where a young prince, now a king, invited four kids (VKs) from the Isle of the Lost to attend school with Auradon kids (AKs) and prove they could fit in. They did. In fact, they fit in so well that King Ben agreed to welcome four new VKs to Auradon Prep.

Now that Mal, Evie, and Jay have graduated (Carlos still has his senior year ahead), the future looks promising for all four VKs. Mal has found true love with King Ben and made it her job to protect her new home of Auradon, Evie is running a successful designer clothing line, Jay is heading to college, and Carlos (along with his best friend, Dude) looks forward to enjoying senior year with his girlfriend, Jane. Will you fit in at Auradon Prep? Step into its hallowed halls, where the descendants of famous fairy-tale heroes and villains attend school together. Meet the students (including newcomers Dizzy, Celia, Squeaky, and Squirmy), decorate your dorm room, design wicked outfits, and feel like you're a member of the Auradon student body.

You'll be . . .

· designing outfits;
· coloring designs and creating your own wickedly awesome doodles;
· solving puzzles, playing games, and even making origami;
· drawing or painting on pages, gluing things, cutting things out . . . you get the idea.

This is YOUR book, made just for you.

ARE YOU AN AK OR A VK?

At first, the VKs found that fitting in with the Auradon kids wasn't as easy as they'd thought it would be. No wonder. AKs are cheerful and kind, and they love doing good deeds. VKs aren't taught to be like that at all. They're rotten and evil, and they love getting into mischief.

So how about you? Are you more like an AK or a VK? Answer the questions to find out!

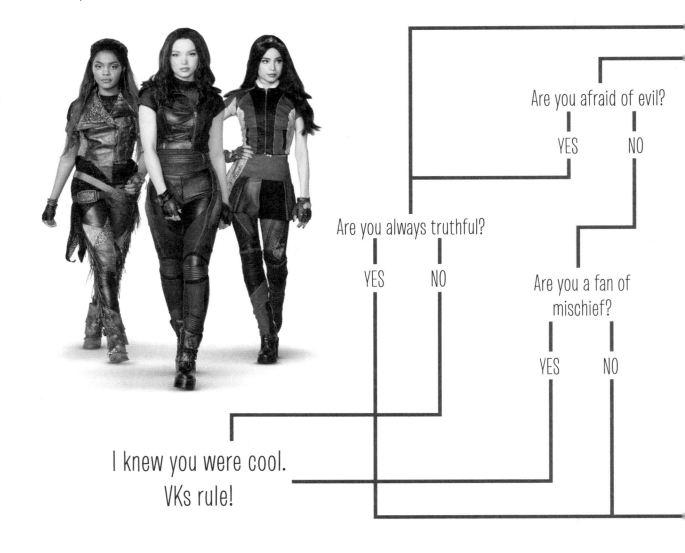

Are you afraid of evil?

YES   NO

Are you always truthful?

YES   NO

Are you a fan of mischief?

YES   NO

I knew you were cool.
VKs rule!

START HERE!

Do you dream about world domination?

YES

NO

Do you ever cheer for the bad guy?

Do you love rainbows?

YES   NO

NO   YES

Have you ever made a
flower arrangement?

Does the phrase
"Oh, how sweet!"
make you gag?

NO   YES

YES   NO

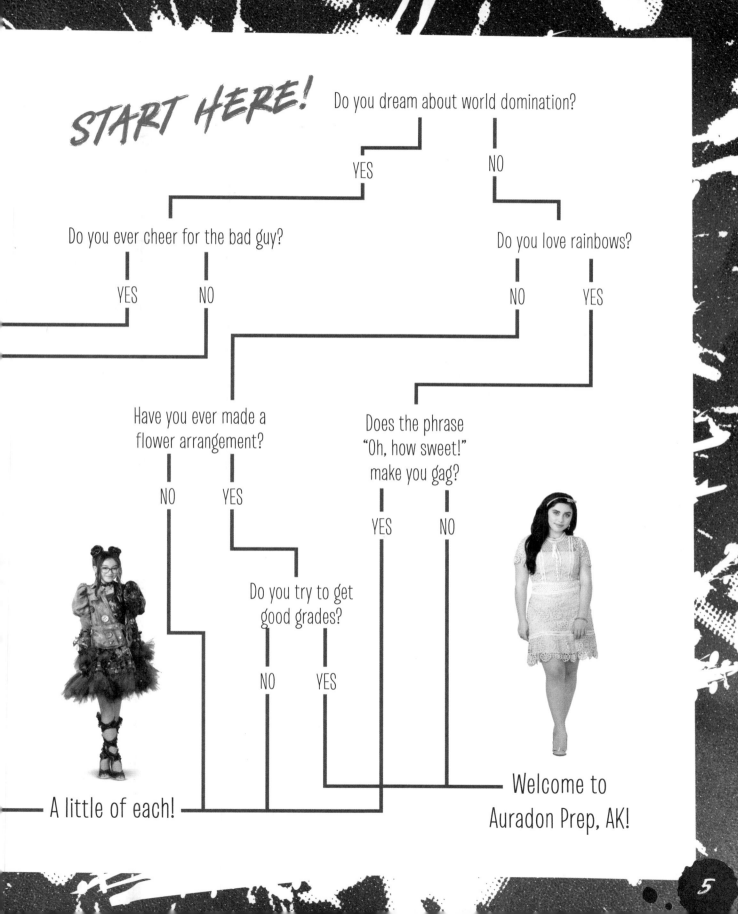

Do you try to get
good grades?

NO   YES

A little of each!

Welcome to
Auradon Prep, AK!

MEET MAL
DAUGHTER OF MALEFICENT

Leader of the VKs

Magical Power: Can transform into a purple dragon

Special Talent: Graffiti artist

Most Likely To: Become queen

RIDING IN STYLE

Mal zips around Auradon City on this purple scooter King Ben gave her.
Use stickers to decorate it any way you like.

BEWARE, FORSWEAR . . . .

Magic is frowned upon in Auradon, but Mal has never been one to play by the rules. She no longer relies on her spell book for incantations, but the daughter of Maleficent has been known to cast an occasional spell, especially when it's needed to keep Auradon and the people she loves safe.

This puzzle contains twelve words, all of which have something to do with magic. They can be found running across, up, down, diagonally, and even backward! Circle each word you find. When you're done, jot down the blue letters that appear inside circled words and unscramble them on the next page. Get it right and you'll be chillin' like a villain!

```
I  N  V  I  S  I  B  L  E  G
T  S  Q  H  N  M  B  U  C  F
N  W  I  T  C  H  V  C  K  G
O  A  C  T  R  I  C  K  L  O
I  N  O  O  B  U  A  N  P  B
T  D  B  M  N  S  P  E  L  L
O  F  W  O  L  J  Q  R  N  E
P  E  I  N  A  M  U  L  E  T
D  R  A  G  O  N  A  R  P  B
C  P  R  O  R  R  I  M  E  K
```

AMULET
CONJURE
DRAGON
GOBLET
INVISIBLE
LUCK
MIRROR
POTION
SPELL
TRICK
WAND
WITCH

_ _ _ _ _ _ _ _

MAL'S SPELLS

Mal used to turn to her spell book for everything. Not anymore! However, on the rare occasion, she does use magic to help her and her friends in times of need. Using the key on the right, see if you can decode her next spell.

PAPER DRAGON

Mal feels responsible for protecting Auradon and the people she loves. When evil comes to town, she transforms into a giant purple dragon to battle villains and keep her home safe. For a little dragon-inspired crafting, make one of these origami dragon heads!

TIP: Press your creases down flat.

Follow these steps:

1. Fold a square sheet of craft paper in half in two directions.
2. Fold in half in two other directions.
3. Fold the two side corners down to the bottom, then fold the top corner down, too.
4. Fold the bottom corner of the top flap up.
5. Fold the two outside corners into the middle.
6. Fold the top corner down.
7. Turn over the paper. Repeat steps 4, 5, and 6.
8. To open the dragon's head, pull it gently from the sides.

Decorate the head with markers, paint, feathers, glitter, and other art supplies!

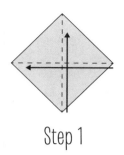

Step 1　　　　　Step 2

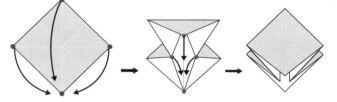

Step 3

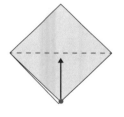 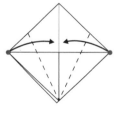   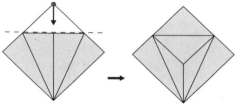

Step 4　　　　Step 5　　　　Step 6

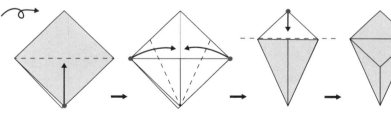

Step 7

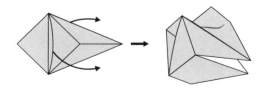

Step 8

13

MEET EVIE

DAUGHTER OF THE EVIL QUEEN

Mal's best friend and owner of Evie's 4 Hearts

Favorite Cause: Bringing new VKs to Auradon Prep

Brought from the Isle: Her mother's magic mirror

Most Likely To: Run a fashion empire

ACCESSORY DESIGNER

Use stickers to help Evie transform this basic handbag into a wickedly cool designer purse.

WICKEDLY GOOD WARDROBE

Evie wants something new to wear on her next date with Doug. She's so busy designing dresses for her Evie's 4 Hearts fashion line that she doesn't have time to work on an outfit for herself!

Evie likes to be girly but adds fashionable edginess to her outfits with graffiti-inspired colors, leather accents, and metal studs. Design a new look for Evie that fits her style, and include every detail: even nail polish can make a big difference to an outfit.

EVIE'S 4 HEARTS

MEET JAY

SON OF JAFAR

Star athlete of Auradon Prep's tourney and swords and shields teams

Villainous Traits Used for Good: Agility and sleight of hand (learned as a thief) to win on the tourney field

Signature Accessory: Knit beanie

Most Likely To: Play college sports

LOCKER DECORATOR

Jay's locker needs some decorating. Use stickers to make his plain locker wickedly cool.

ESCAPE FROM THE ISLE OF THE LOST

When Mal, Evie, Ben, Carlos, and Jay go to the Isle of the Lost to pick up the new VKs, Jay is in the driver's seat. Now that they've picked up Dizzy, Celia, Squeaky, and Squirmy, help Jay navigate the Auradon limo safely off the Isle.

START

FINISH

See answer key on page 88.

MEET CARLOS

SON OF CRUELLA DE VIL

Once afraid of dogs, and now an aspiring vet

Favorite Food: Chocolate

Special Talent: Tech-savvy computer guru

Most Likely To: Rescue a dozen dogs

THE PERFECT PRESENT

Carlos is excited about giving his girlfriend, Jane, her birthday gift. Help him decorate the gift box using stickers, markers, or whatever you'd like.

OVERCOMING YOUR FEARS

When Carlos lived on the Isle, he was afraid of a lot of things: his mom, talking to girls, and especially dogs! But once he got to Auradon and met Dude, he realized his mom had exaggerated, and he figured out that dogs aren't so bad after all. With Jay's help, he found a way to talk to girls—make that Jane. However, he admits he's still a little afraid to tell his mom he wants to become a vet.

What about you? Have you ever been afraid of something? Make a list of ways to conquer your fears!

_____

_____

_____

_____

_____

_____

_____

_____

_____

_____

_____

_____

_____

_____

CARLOS OVERCAME HIS FEARS BY . . .
* listening to his instincts,
* getting advice from trusted friends, and
* being himself!

MEET DIZZY

DAUGHTER OF DRIZELLA AND GRANDDAUGHTER OF LADY TREMAINE

Talented hairstylist and designer

Before Coming to Auradon: Worked at the Curl Up and Dye salon

Moment That Changed Everything: Seeing her headpiece designs for Cotillion on TV

Most Likely To: Follow in Evie's footsteps

DARING HAIR

Dizzy's hair accessories are super creative. Design your own awesome headpiece using the stickers in this book!

Use the tiara as a base to create a wickedly cool hair accessory that is stylish and showcases your creativity. If you're at all like Dizzy, the wilder the better!

PERFECT PURPLE PIGMENT

When Mal desperately needs a touch-up on her signature purple tresses, she trusts no one more than Dizzy. After all, Dizzy essentially ran her grandmother's beauty salon, Curl Up and Dye, on the Isle, and she came up with Evie's crown braids. Mal is on her way to see Dizzy, and Dizzy can't find the perfect purple pigment! Can you help her?

Dizzy does remember that . . .

- the correct jar is above a jar with no lid.
- the correct jar is between a jar with red hair dye and a tall jar.
- the correct jar does not have a cloth top.

NAILED IT!

What's your favorite look for your nails? Dizzy paints each of her nails a different color or pattern. Jane and Audrey stick with pink. Evie and Mal go for fashionably evil with dark purple, magenta, or black.

Try out some new ideas here. Sketch patterns on the nails to the right and use markers to fill them in. Then try them for real!

IF YOU NEED SOME INSPIRATION, YOU CAN TAKE CUES FROM THESE PATTERNS! JUST ADD COLOR.

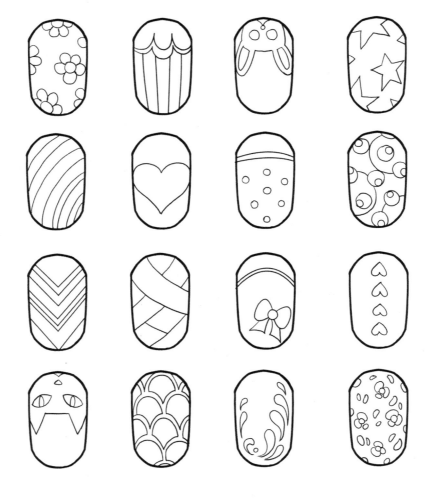

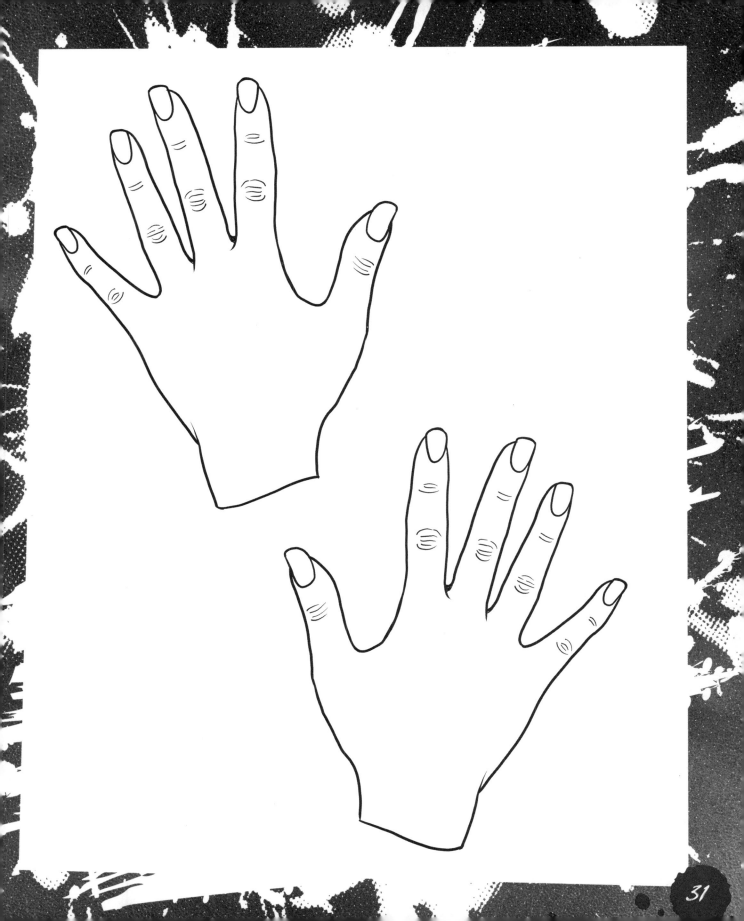

DIZZY'S PAINTED NAILS GAME

Help Dizzy come up with some wild nail polish combinations by playing this game. Gather some friends and try it out.

1. Photocopy the game board and arrow on stiff paper.
2. Use colorful markers to decorate the game board. You can also write game play directions in some of the squares, like Spin Again; Paint 2 Nails; Choose Your Color; Paint 1 Nail on Your Friend.
3. Cut out the arrow and attach it to the center of the board with a paper fastener.
4. Place different colors of nail polish on each dot.
5. To play, take turns spinning the arrow. Paint the color it points to on one nail. Keep going until all fingernails and toenails are painted!

TIP: Best for two to four players.

DIZZY'S PAINTED NAILS GAME

33

MEET CELIA

DAUGHTER OF DR. FACILIER

Sassy, fearless daddy's girl enjoying the journey

Special Skill: Fortune-telling

Side Hustle: Errand rat for Hades

Most Likely To: Tell you what she's really thinking

BLING COLLECTOR

Celia has been admiring the way Auradon girls add bling to their fashions. Use stickers to stock Celia's jewelry box with the latest accessories you think she'd like.

WHAT'S IN THE CARDS?

Celia uses her fortune cards to read the future. Will you meet a handsome prince? Does an adventurous journey lie ahead? Your future may be in her cards.

Create a new fortune card for Celia's deck. It can be a card that predicts a future you dream of, one that foreshadows a mischievous event, or whatever you want!

MEET SQUEAKY AND SQUIRMY

TWIN SONS OF SMEE

Shy, quiet brothers determined to change their destiny

Who's Older: Squeaky, by four minutes

What They Won't Miss About the Isle: Pirates

Most Likely To: Always stick together

REUNITE THE TWINS

Squeaky and Squirmy don't like to be apart for very long. Help them find their way back to each other.

WHO YOU ARE IS WHO YOU NEED TO BE

Squeaky and Squirmy didn't exactly fit in at the Isle of the Lost's docks. Their father, Smee, knew they could have a better life in Auradon, so he encouraged them to apply to Auradon Prep, where they could succeed by just being themselves.

Make a collage of your favorite things and display it in your personal space to remind you to stay positive and true to yourself, because being different and standing out is way more fun than blending in!

1. Gather pictures of things that make you smile or remind you of a good time. You can use a combination of photos, cutouts from magazines, objects, fabric, stickers, markers, and paint . . . whatever inspires you.
2. Need some ideas? How about including your friends, family, pets, vacation pictures, and favorite foods, colors, toys, and movies?
3. Consider adding slips of paper with inspiring words or sayings, like Follow Your Dreams; Be Good, Be Brave, Be Free; Rise Up and Shine; Who You Are Is Who You Need to Be; Good Is the New Bad; Happily Ever After with a Little Flavor!
4. Arrange everything on a poster board in a creative pattern. Don't be afraid to overlap and put things at different angles.
5. Use all-purpose glue to hold it all together, and let it dry for several hours before hanging it up.
6. If you want, frame your collage for a really finished look.

 TIP: If you do use a frame, make sure you cut your poster board to fit before you start assembling your collage.

Here are some sayings to get you started! Photocopy this page
before coloring them. Cut them out and use them in your collage!

MEET UMA

DAUGHTER OF URSULA

Leader of the Isle of the Lost pirates

Magic Power: Can transform into a giant octopus

Favorite Accessory: Her mother's shell necklace

Most Likely To: Become ambassador of the Isle

MEET HARRY

SON OF CAPTAIN HOOK

Uma's pirate first lieutenant

Signature Accessory:
A silver hook

Fashion Statement: A little
eyeliner can be very masculine.

Most Likely To: "Borrow" money
from you

MEET GIL

SON OF GASTON

The muscle of Uma's pirate gang

Surprising Trait: He's a hugger.

Favorite New Snack: Fruit

Most Likely To: Meet a penguin

MAKE THE ISLE A BETTER PLACE

The Isle of the Lost needs some sprucing up! Use stickers, markers, paint, and whatever else you can get your hands on to design a new and improved Isle street.

ARE YOU ROTTEN TO THE CORE?

Every villain kid who goes to Auradon Prep eventually has to face the question *Is this where I truly belong?* When your whole life has been spent fending for yourself and proving you're evil, it can be tough fitting into a world that expects the complete opposite!

Where would you fit in best—Auradon or the Isle? Take this quiz to find out! Circle your answers.

1. Which of these jobs would you NOT want?
   a. Royal guard
   b. Barrier maintenance technician
   c. Teacher at Auradon Prep
   d. Shopkeeper on the Isle

2. How clean do you like your room to be?
   a. Who cares?
   b. Straightened up.
   c. I don't.
   d. I want it to sparkle!

3. Being caught in a thunderstorm at night is . . .
   a. awesome.
   b. scary.
   c. a good opportunity for mischief.
   d. a good way to catch a cold.

4. When someone tells you the rules of a game, what do you do?
   a. Immediately think of ways to bend the rules.
   b. Think, "Well, that sounds fair."
   c. Trick your opponent!
   d. Decide to do your best!

5. Which of these would be your favorite way to get around?
   a. Trash truck
   b. Purple scooter
   c. Pirate ship
   d. Limo

6. Which of these makes you happiest?
   a. A dark alley
   b. A rainbow
   c. Being by yourself
   d. Going to a party

7. The Isle of the Lost is . . .
   a. not so bad.
   b. a prison.
   c. misunderstood.
   d. dangerous.

8. Where would you want to live?
   a. A hideout
   b. A dorm room
   c. Somewhere gloomy
   d. A sunny beach

If you circled mostly As and Cs:

You're someone who finds the VILLAIN KID lifestyle kind of cool and might want to give it a try. A hideout in the dark heart of a forbidden island is right up your alley!

If you circled mostly Bs and Ds:

You're way more suited to the lifestyle of an AURADON KID. They have the chance to follow their dreams and make the most of every opportunity.

MEET KING BEN

SON OF BEAST AND BELLE

King of the United States of Auradon

First Initiative as King: Inviting VKs to Auradon Prep

Best Gift He Has Ever Given: A purple scooter (to Mal)

Most Likely To: Always see the best in everyone

Help King Ben write an official welcome letter for the new villain kids.

A RING FIT FOR A KING

King Ben's crown and ring both have images of his dad, Beast, to represent his royal family. If Ben could choose his own ring, what do you think it would look like? Would he incorporate a design inspired by his mother, Belle? Or would he add something to represent his love for Mal? Design a ring you think Ben would wear.

MEET JANE

Friendly, outgoing AK who's welcoming to all

Special Talent: Best party planner in Auradon

Hometown: Born and raised in Auradon City

Most Likely To: Plan a royal event

52

PICTURE-PERFECT PARTY

Use stickers, markers, fabric swatches, and more to transform this empty table into a tempting party spread. Add decorations, food, a centerpiece, or whatever you'd like.

PARTY PLANNER

Jane is known for planning the best parties in Auradon. That includes invitations, decorations, a menu, party favors, flowers, lighting. . . . The list goes on and on. She knows that even though it's a lot of work, an awesome party is a great way for everyone to celebrate.

What would be the perfect way for your family or friends to gather together and celebrate? Is it a party, an adventure, or a big dinner? Will there be decorations, gifts, food, entertainment? Share your ideas with others and maybe you can make your dream party a reality!

MY PARTY PLAN

When & Where

Who's Coming

Food & Drinks

Sweets

Music

Decorations

Fun Stuff

Party Favors

_____

_____

PARTY INVITATIONS

Party invitations are a must for any kind of gathering. Jane knows the perfect invitation doesn't just look good; it has all the information the guests will need. Here are six tips for easy-and awesome-party invitations.

- DO use the invitation template to the right.

- DO decorate the invitation with stickers from this book.

- DO fill in all the blanks EXCEPT the "To" line.

- DO make color photocopies: one for each person you're inviting.

- DO cut out the invitations. Now fill in the "To" line.

- DON'T send them out too late! Two weeks ahead of time is perfect.

PARTY TIME!

TO

_____

A PARTY FOR

_____

WHEN

_____

WHERE

_____

WHAT TO WEAR

_____

CAN YOU MAKE IT? LET ME KNOW BY CALLING

_____

MEET AUDREY

DAUGHTER OF AURORA AND
GRANDDAUGHTER OF QUEEN LEAH

Perfect princess still trying to discover her destiny

Former Boyfriends: King Ben and Chad Charming

Hobbies: Cheerleading, going to spas, and writing in her journal

Most Likely To: Wear pink

ACCESSORIZE AUDREY

Audrey loves to dress up, and as every princess knows, the right jewelry and accessories can make an outfit truly special. What pieces would you add to Audrey's outfit? Draw the items you think she'd like.

PLAN FOR YOUR DREAMS!

AKs, like Audrey, have always been taught to set goals that will help them achieve their dreams.

What are your goals? What do you do each day to reach them? A daily journal can help you stay on track. Write out your goals here, separating them into *immediate goals* and *long-term goals*. Put each list in order from most important to least important.

Think about starting a journal to track your progress and collect keepsakes. If you already have one, keep going!

IMMEDIATE GOALS

Make my dream come true, whatever it takes.

_____

_____

_____

_____

_____

_____

_____

_____

LONG-TERM GOALS

Dream up a new Happily Ever After.

_____

_____

_____

_____

_____

_____

_____

_____

_____

_____

_____

_____

MEET DOUG

SON OF DOPEY

Smart and sweet leader of the school band

After-School Activity: Helping Evie with her company's accounting

Favorite Instrument: All of them

Most Likely To: Play a set with the Dragon Slayers

IT ALL STARTED IN CHEMISTRY

Doug and Evie discovered the formula for true love when they first met in chemistry. Piece together their picture using stickers in this book to see the happy couple today.

MEET CHAD

SON OF CINDERELLA AND PRINCE CHARMING

Preppy prince missing the chivalry gene

Special Trait: Great sense of style

Favorite pastimes: Sports and taking selfies

Most Likely To: Move home to his parents' castle after graduation

PRINCE OF STYLE

The way Chad dresses may scream AK, but he has always been open to experimenting with fashion. Design a new look for this preppy prince using stickers, markers, paints, scraps of fabric, and glue.

AURADON KNIGHTS R.O.A.R.

Chad is a proud member of the Auradon Knights swords and shields team. Now that he's graduating, he wants a new sword designed just for him.

Draw a sword that says something about his family history and personality. You can add jewels, words etched into the metal, and even patterns to make the sword unique.

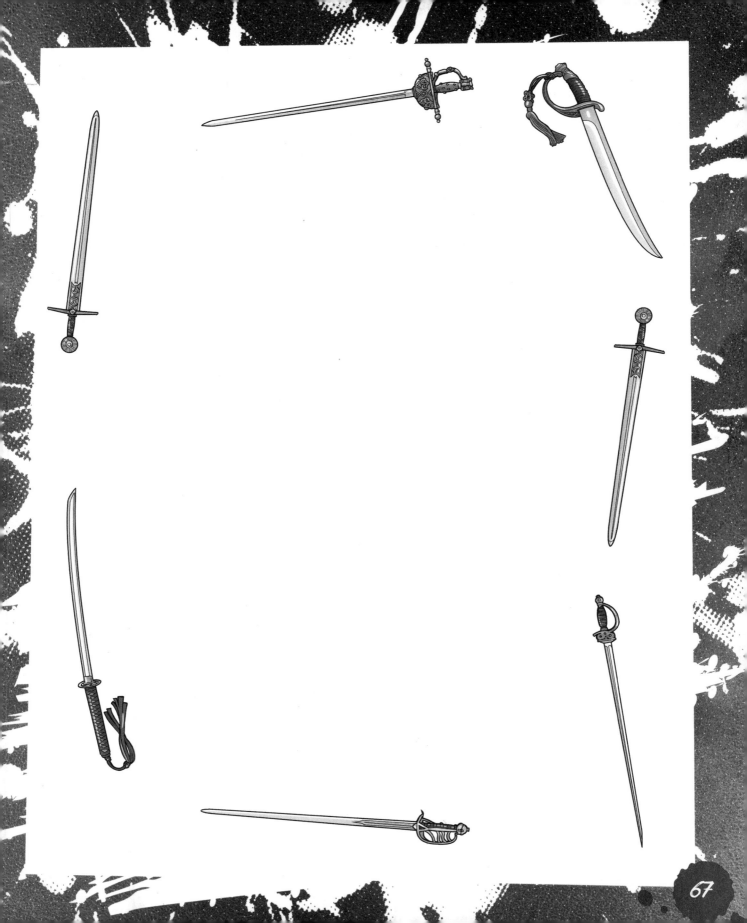

WHICH CHARACTER ARE YOU?

Each VK has a distinct style and personality.
Which one are you most similar to? Take this quiz to find
out, circling your answers.

1. What's your favorite color?
   - a. Purple
   - b. Turquoise
   - c. Bright blue
   - d. All of them!

2. What is your favorite hobby?
   - a. Graffiti
   - b. Bossing people around
   - c. Designing clothes
   - d. Coming up with new hairstyles

3. On a Friday night, you can be found . . .
   - a. memorizing spells.
   - b. waiting tables.
   - c. starting your own business.
   - d. cleaning your grandmother's shop.

4. Your style is . . .
   - a. bold, with lots of leather.
   - b. inspired by the ocean.
   - c. edgy but feminine.
   - d. colorful!

5. You'd prefer to live in . . .
   - a. your secret hideout.
   - b. a ship.
   - c. a castle.
   - d. Auradon, someday.

6. Your favorite accessory is . . .
   - a. a spell book.
   - b. a shell necklace.
   - c. a magic mirror.
   - d. headphones.

7. Your friends would describe you as . . .
   - a. a natural leader.
   - b. What friends? You have minions.
   - c. loyal and smart.
   - d. creative and colorful.

8. Your favorite catchphrase:
   - a. Long live evil!
   - b. What's my name?
   - c. Magic mirror . . .
   - d. You can take the girl out of the Isle, but you can't take the Isle out of the girl!

If you circled mostly As:
You'd wear purple all the time if you could, and you know the power of magic. Sometimes you have a hard time fitting in, but like Mal, you're lucky to have friends who remind you you're perfect just the way you are.

If you circled mostly Bs:
Just like Uma, you fear nothing and no one. You know that if anyone tests your power, your gang will always back you up. But is bossing around your minions the best use of your desire to lead?

If you circled mostly Cs:
You know that a great outfit can brighten any day, and you enjoy designing your own clothes. You're independent and a loyal friend—just like Evie.

If you circled mostly Ds:
Your creative energy is always leading you to make crazy and wild things—with lots of color and plenty of style! You're never afraid to try something new and bold, but just like Dizzy, you dream of a bigger and better place.

WHAT DEFINES YOU?

Many of the Descendants have iconic elements that show up in their clothing to represent their families or personalities: Ben's crown and ring feature the Beast; Mal's clothes sometimes incorporate dragon-inspired patterns; Evie's clothes have hearts sewn on them to represent her business; and Uma's outfits are turquoise and pirate-like to remind her of the ocean.

Design a symbol that defines you! Get inspiration from the talents and interests you and your family have. Do you love music? Maybe you want to use a treble clef. Into sports? How about including a soccer ball? Celebrate what you're passionate about!

Take it one step further and put your designed symbol on a large poster or a banner made of a piece of thick light-colored material. Hang it in your locker or on your bedroom wall—with an adult's help, of course!

HOW WELL DO YOU KNOW THE AKs AND THE VKs?

All the Auradon kids and villain kids have their own treasured or magical items they just can't do without. On the next page, draw a line to connect each item to its owner.

SHARD OF MAGIC MIRROR   UMA

HOOK   EVIE

SPELL BOOK   BEN

SWORD   DIZZY

SHELL NECKLACE   MAL

3-D PRINTER   CARLOS

CROWN   CELIA

GLUE GUN   LONNIE

FORTUNE-TELLING CARDS   HARRY

73

See answer key on page 88.

APPLY TO AURADON PREP

Fill out this application to be considered for admission to Auradon Prep.

APPLICATION *for* AURADON PREP

Children of the Isle of the Lost! Mal and King Ben invite you to meet them and the other villain kids formerly of the Isle at Auradon Prep to enroll you for the upcoming scholastic year. By filling out this application form you will be eligible to become part of the second wave of villain kids that will help to reunite our divided kingdom.

Please complete this form as accurately as you can. Our goal is to welcome all of the children of the Isle of the Lost to Auradon as expeditiously as possible. At this time, however, we will only be accepting four more. Mal and King Ben ask you to be truthful, sincere and to always speak from your heart. In time, we will all be together as one nation. Your courage in volunteering for this program will bring that day closer! Best of luck!

_____
Name

_____
Known aliases

_____
Nicknames or other

_____
Date of birth or best guess

*Please place
photo here*

_____
Place of birth

_____
Favorite color

_____
Favorite activity

_____
Favorite school subject

_____
Parents' names (or aliases)

_____
Parents' profession(s)

Who is your favorite of the first wave of VKs? There is no wrong answer.

_____
_____
_____
_____

In your own words, tell us why you want to come to Auradon. There is no wrong answer.

_____

_____

_____

_____

_____

_____

_____

_____

_____

_____

_____

_____

_____

_____

_____

_____

_____

_____

_____

_____

_____

_____

_____

_____

_____

_____

_____

Congratulations on completing the application. Mal, Jay, Evie, and Carlos will collect it on the appointed date and announce the next of many villain kids who will join them in Auradon. If you are not picked, please don't despair. In time all of you will join us and help make our world whole again!

_____

Signature

Please place thumbprint here

If you were going to redecorate your dorm room, what would you do?
Re-cover the furniture and other surfaces by gluing on scraps of fabric or construction paper. Add stickers and design details. Color the space, draw patterns, and make this room your own.

SIGNATURE LOOK

Want to stand out in the halls of Auradon Prep? Create your own stylish look by designing a signature fabric. Start with your favorite colors, then think of patterns and designs that express your inner self. Use these spaces to experiment with various colors and shapes.

DESIGN YOUR OUTFITS

From going to class and hanging out with friends to attending sporting events and formal dances, there are so many fun activities and events at Auradon Prep. But what will you wear? Use stickers, markers, paints, scraps of fabric, and glue to design some different looks. Show how wickedly cool you can be!

SCHOOL OUTFIT

COTILLION FORMAL WEAR

CLOTHES FOR HANGING WITH FRIENDS

SPORTY ENSEMBLE

THE MAGIC IS IN THE DETAILS

Uma's shell necklace, which came straight from her mom, Ursula, has magical powers outside the barrier. Hades has a magical ember, which he let Mal use to defeat villains in Auradon. How would you design a magical accessory of your own? Draw your ideas in the space provided. Will it have jewels? Secret compartments? Is it surprisingly simple, or is it outrageous? What powers does it have—and more important, how would you use it?

You can use markers or paints. Take it further by gluing on random items, like an old key, a coin, a pebble, a ring, or a feather, as if they were charms. Get creative.

MY ITEM'S MAGICAL POWERS

HOW I'LL USE MY POWERS

FAMILY AND FRIENDSHIPS

Once they got to Auradon, the VKs realized they had to stick together and formed a family-like bond.

What does your friendship tree look like? Fill in the blanks and glue in mini photos of you and your friends wherever you can.

Use scrapbooking supplies, like colored or patterned paper, stickers, lace, ribbon, buttons, and dried flowers, to decorate the page.

AURADON GOES ISLE

Now that VKs are part of the Auradon Prep student body, how would you update the school crest? Create a new crest that represents both Auradon and the Isle, mixing colors and styles to celebrate all that Auradon Prep stands for!

ANSWER KEY

Pages 8-9

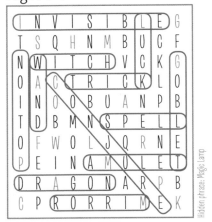

Hidden phrase: Magic Lamp

Pages 10-11
Read it fast at lightning speed.
Remember everything I need.

Pages 20-21

Pages 28-29

Page 39

Pages 72-73

SHARD OF MAGIC MIRROR: EVIE

HOOK: HARRY

SPELL BOOK: MAL

SWORD: LONNIE

SHELL NECKLACE: UMA

3-D PRINTER: CARLOS

CROWN: BEN

GLUE GUN: DIZZY

FORTUNE-TELLING CARDS: CELIA